Licensed exclusively to Top That Publishing Ltd
Tide Mill Way, Woodbridge, Suffolk, IP12 1AP, UK
www.topthatpublishing.com
Copyright © 2016 Tide Mill Media
All rights reserved
0 2 4 6 8 9 7 5 3 1
Manufactured in China

Written by Joshua George
Illustrated by Jennie Poh

ISBN 978-1-78700-467-2

A catalogue record for this book is available from the British Library

'For Lila and her sweet tooth'

Jellyfish are DISGUSTING!

Written by
Joshua George

Illustrated by
Jennie Poh

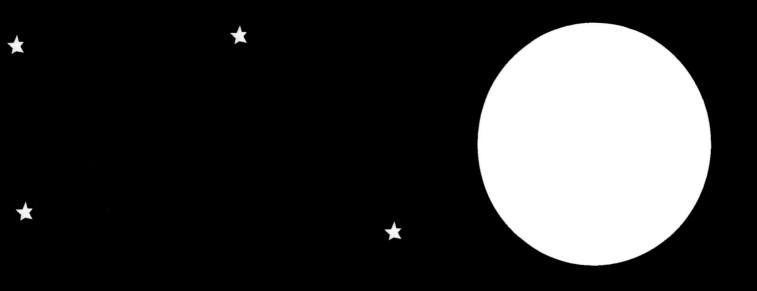

one of nature's most incredible miracles was appearing ...

and his name was BURT!

'I'm not eating jellyfish!' said Burt.
'They are stingy, and stringy
and DISGUSTING!'

'Well, what are you
going to eat then?'
asked his mum.

Burt thought for a minute ... 'Jelly'.

Burt's mum groaned, and with a slow flap of her flippers she soared away after a group of jellyfish.

'Everybody knows turtles eat jellyfish,' she called back, '... you'll see!'

Burt had decided that he would only eat jelly, so jelly would be what he ate! It couldn't be that hard ... all he had to do was find a birthday party, and there must be plenty of those!

Burt began to swim around the seaweed, looking for birthday parties, until finally, he found one ...

'Hey, Tuna,' said Burt, 'Happy Birthday!'

'You look tasty,' said the tuna. 'Can I eat you?'

'**No,**' said Burt, slowly and clearly.
'It would be VERY RUDE to eat
someone who's come to
wish you a happy birthday!'

The tuna shrugged. 'OK,'
he said, 'welcome to the party.'

Burt went straight over to the jelly and ate as much as his little belly could hold.

Above a colourful reef, Burt found a manta ray having a party
with all his manta ray friends. They were spinning
and twirling slowly and gracefully.
'Hey, Manta Ray,' said Burt,
'Happy Birthday!'

'Wooooh,' whirled the manta ray.
'Welcome to the party!'

And Burt ate as much jelly as
his little belly could hold.

Near big cliffs where waves crashed and boomed, Burt saw a seal having a birthday party with all his seal friends. They were playing hide-and-seek in the rock caves.

'Hey, Seal,' said Burt,
'Happy Birthday!'

'Shhhh ...'
whispered the seal,
'I'm playing hide-and-seek!
But welcome to the party!'

And Burt ate as much jelly
as his little belly could hold.

At the edge of the deep water, where the ocean grew so dark that you couldn't see to the bottom, Burt met a dolphin and a whale having a joint birthday party.

'Hey, Dolphin, hey Whale,'
said Burt, 'Happy Birthday!'

'**Wheeeee!**' twirled the dolphin,
leaping and spinning. 'Thanks!'

'Welcome to the party,' said the whale
as he sped towards the surface.
'**Watch out!**'

And so Burt spent his days
searching the big, wide ocean
for birthday parties.

He saw all kinds of wonderful things,
and met all kinds of friendly creatures,
and he ate all kinds of lovely jelly ...

But it wasn't always easy finding a birthday party, and some days Burt was very hungry indeed.

One such hungry day, Burt couldn't believe his eyes. His friends had arranged a surprise birthday party just for him!

'We know how much you love birthday parties!' said Tuna.

'And everybody knows turtles eat jellyfish,' said Dolphin, 'so we found you a really big juicy one!'

Burt swallowed and looked at his friends.
They looked back at him, excitedly.

'Go on,' said Dolphin. 'Don't be shy!'

Burt closed his eyes and took a bite.
Slowly, he started to chew.

'Umm, that's not
so bad!' he said,
with his mouth full.

'Is there
any more?'

So Burt's jelly-eating days were over, and he spent his time following jellyfish across the open ocean. There were always other turtles to meet, and interesting things to see.

Burt stopped by to see his old friends from time to time, although gradually there were fewer and fewer of them left.

Turtles live for many, many years and the truth was, Burt was getting old.

Burt was passing as one of nature's most incredible miracles was appearing ...

'I'm not eating jellyfish! They are stingy, and stringy and **DISGUSTING!**' said a baby turtle.

'Everybody knows turtles eat jellyfish,' called Burt as he swam past, '... you'll see!'